# BUTTERFLIES

Dad is busy in the backyard with Bluey and Bingo when their neighbour Judo appears.
"What are you doing, Bluey's dad?" she asks.
"Just putting up a fabric swing," he says.

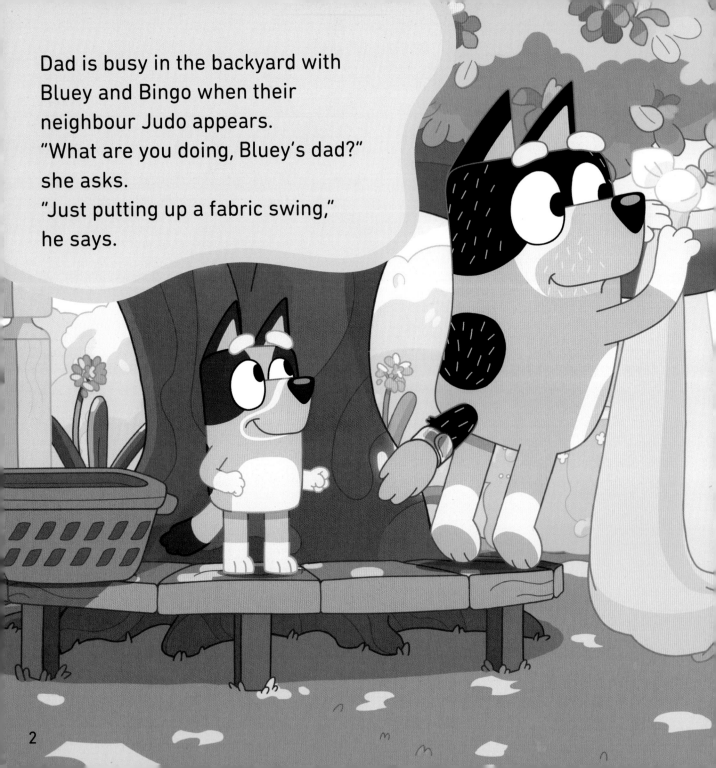

"Yeah, they have them
at Bluey's school," Bingo
tells Judo.
"I know that!" Judo replies.
"Bluey's MY friend!"

3

They decide to play Butterflies, so Bluey explains the rules.

"OK, first the caterpillar crawls along the ground."

"Then it gets in the cocoon."

"Then it hatches as a butterfly."

"But the butterfly catchers have been hiding . . ."

". . . and **CATCH** it!"

"Ooh, can I be the caterpillar first?" asks Bingo.
But Judo has other ideas.

I'M GOING FIRST!

Bluey and Bingo find
somewhere to hide.
"Judo is so bossy," sighs Bingo.

Suddenly, she spots a ladybug.
"Ooh!" she says and starts to sing.

♫♪

POOR LITTLE BUG
ON THE WALL
DING! CHING!
NO ONE TO LOVE
HIM AT ALL
DING! CHING!
NO ONE TO TICKLE
HIS TOES
DING! CHING!
NO ONE TO BLOW
HIS NOSE...

♫♪

Judo hatches as a butterfly . . .

. . . and the butterfly catchers chase her down.

Next it's Bingo's turn.
"You're too small to be a caterpillar," says Judo.
"No I'm not!" Bingo replies.
"Go on, Bingo. We'll be the butterfly catchers," says Bluey.

Bluey and Judo run off to hide while Bingo crawls into her cocoon.

"Little kids take **SO LONG** to do everything!" complains Judo.
"She's only got little legs," says Bluey.

"Hey, Bluey," whispers Judo. "Let's run away from Bingo."
"What? Why?" asks Bluey.
"She's taking ages," says Judo.

Judo runs away.

Bluey thinks about it.

She runs away from Bingo too.

WAIT FOR ME!

Bingo climbs out of the cocoon
and flaps around the backyard.
"Ooh, look at me.
I'm a butterfly!"

FLAP!
FLAP!

HOPE THERE'S
NO BUTTERFLY
CATCHERS NEARBY!

Bingo looks everywhere,
but Bluey and Judo are
nowhere to be seen.

Eventually Bingo finds them. They are playing
a different game without her.
"Bluey, you were meant to catch me!" says Bingo.

"Ahh! Quick, Bluey, run away!" says Judo.
Bluey runs away again, leaving Bingo alone.

15

Bingo crawls back into the cocoon. She sings sadly . . .

POOR LITTLE BUG
ON THE WALL.
DING. CHING.

NO ONE TO LOVE
HIM AT ALL.
DING. CHING.

Bluey feels bad.

"I might go and see if Bingo's all right," she says.
"She'll be fine," Judo tells her. "Let's play Phones!"

RING!
RING!

Bluey starts playing,
but she is worried
about Bingo.

HI, IT'S ME
JUDO . . .

JUDO, I THINK
I NEED TO
FIND BINGO.

She tries to tell Judo, but
Judo's not listening.

LET ME TELL
YOU ALL ABOUT
MY DAY . . .

OK THEN,
I'M GOING
NOW. BYE.

Bluey finds Bingo in the swing.

"I'm sorry, Bingo. I didn't mean to run away from you. Judo made me do it," says Bluey. "Well, she didn't **MAKE** me do it. I did it a bit myself."

But Bingo doesn't answer.

19

"I'll never do it again," Bluey promises.
"Please can we play together?"

But Bingo still doesn't answer.

"*Poor little bug on the wall,
Ding Ching,*" Bluey sings.
"*No one to love her at all . . .*"

DING!
CHING!

21

RING!
RING!

Suddenly, they hear Judo looking for them.
"Quick, hide!" says Bingo.

Bluey climbs into the cocoon with Bingo.

"There you are!
You ran away
from me."

"Well, you ran away from me!" Bingo replies.
"New rule," says Bluey. "From now on, no one runs away from anyone, OK?"
Bluey says sorry to Judo for running off.
"I'm sorry too, Bingo," says Judo.

It's time for another game of Butterflies, but Bluey, Bingo and Judo all want to be catchers.
"Who will we catch?" wonders Bluey . . .